THE GINGERBREAD BOY

THE GINGERBREAD BOY

illustrated by

WILLIAM CURTIS HOLDSWORTH

•

FARRAR, STRAUS AND GIROUX · NEW YORK

An Ariel Book

Illustrations Copyright © 1968 by William Curtis Holdsworth
Library of Congress catalog card number 68–23751
ISBN 0-374-32575-8
Printed in the United States of America
Published simultaneously in Canada
Designed by Jane Byers Bierhorst

For E. P.
Mary and Jeannette
●

Once upon a time there were a little old woman and a little old man, and they lived all alone in a little old house. They hadn't any little girls or any little boys at all. So one day the little old woman

made a boy out of gingerbread. She made him a chocolate jacket, and put cinnamon seeds in it for buttons; his eyes were made of fine, fat currants; his mouth was made of rose-colored sugar; and he had a gay little cap of orange sugar candy. When the little old woman

had rolled him out, and dressed him up, and pinched his gingerbread shoes into shape, she put him in a pan. Then she put the pan in the oven and shut the door; and she thought, "Now I shall have a little boy of my own."

When it was time for the Gingerbread Boy to be done, she opened the oven door and pulled out the pan. Out jumped the little

Gingerbread Boy on to the floor, and away he ran, out the door
and down the street. The little old woman and the little old man

ran after him as fast as they could, but he just laughed, and shouted:

"Run! run! as fast as you can!
You can't catch me, I'm the Gingerbread Man!"

And they couldn't catch him.

The little Gingerbread Boy ran on and on, until he came to a cow by the roadside. "Stop, little Gingerbread Boy," said the cow. "I want to eat you." The little Gingerbread Boy laughed, and said:

"I have run away from a little old woman,

And a little old man,

And I can run away from you, I can!"

And as the cow chased him, he looked over his shoulder and cried:

"Run! run! as fast as you can!
You can't catch me, I'm the Gingerbread Man!"

And the cow couldn't catch him.

The little Gingerbread Boy ran on, and on, and on, till he came
to a horse in the pasture. "Please stop, little Gingerbread Boy,"
said the horse. "You look very good to eat." But the little Gingerbread Boy laughed out loud. "O ho! O ho!" he said.

"I have run away from a little old woman,

A little old man,

A cow,

And I can run away from you, I can!"

And as the horse chased him, he looked over his shoulder and cried:

"Run! run! as fast as you can!
You can't catch me, I'm the Gingerbread Man!"

And the horse couldn't catch him.

By and by the little Gingerbread Boy came to a barn full of threshers. When the threshers smelled the Gingerbread Boy, they tried to pick him up, and said, "Don't run so fast, little Gingerbread Boy; you look very good to eat." But the little Gingerbread Boy ran harder than ever, and as he ran he cried out:

"I have run away from a little old woman,
  A little old man,
  A cow,
  A horse,
  And I can run away from you, I can!"

And when he found that he was ahead of the threshers, he turned and shouted back to them:

"Run! run! as fast as you can!
You can't catch me, I'm the Gingerbread Man!"

And the threshers couldn't catch him.

Then the little Gingerbread Boy ran faster than ever. He ran and ran until he came to a field full of mowers. When the mowers saw how fine he looked, they ran after him, calling out, "Wait a bit! Wait a bit, little Gingerbread Boy! We wish to eat you!" But the little Gingerbread Boy laughed harder than ever, and ran like the wind. "O ho! O ho!" he said.

"I have run away from a little old woman,
  A little old man,
  A cow,
  A horse,
  A barn full of threshers,
  And I can run away from you, I can!"

And when he found he was ahead of the mowers, he turned and shouted back to them:

"Run! run! as fast as you can!
You can't catch me, I'm the Gingerbread Man!"

And the mowers couldn't catch him.

By this time the little Gingerbread Boy was so proud that he didn't think anybody could catch him. Pretty soon he saw a fox coming across a field. The fox looked at him and began to run. But the little Gingerbread Boy shouted across to him, "You can't catch me!" The fox began to run faster, and the little Gingerbread Boy ran faster, and as he ran he said:

"I have run away from a little old woman,
A little old man,
A cow,
A horse,
A barn full of threshers,
A field full of mowers,
And I can run away from you, I can!

"Run! run! as fast as you can!
You can't catch me, I'm the Gingerbread Man!"

"Why," said the fox, "I would not catch you if I could. I would not think of disturbing you."

Just then the little Gingerbread Boy came to a river. He could

not swim across, and he wanted to keep running away from the cow
and the horse and the people.

"Jump on my tail and I will take you across," said the fox.

So the Gingerbread Boy jumped on the fox's tail, and the fox swam into the river. A little distance from the shore the fox said,

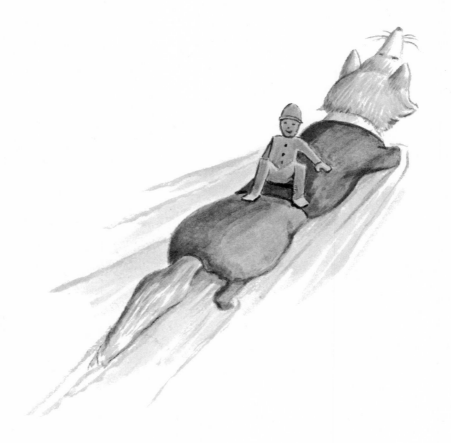

"Little Gingerbread Boy, I think you had better get on my back, or you may fall off."

So the little Gingerbread Boy jumped on his back.

After swimming a little farther, the fox said, "I'm afraid you will get wet there. You had better jump on my shoulder."

So the little Gingerbread Boy jumped on his shoulder.

When they were near the other side of the river, the fox said, "Little Gingerbread Boy, my back is tired. Will you jump on my nose?"

So the little Gingerbread Boy jumped on his nose.

As soon as the fox reached the shore, he threw back his head, and into his mouth fell the little Gingerbread Boy.